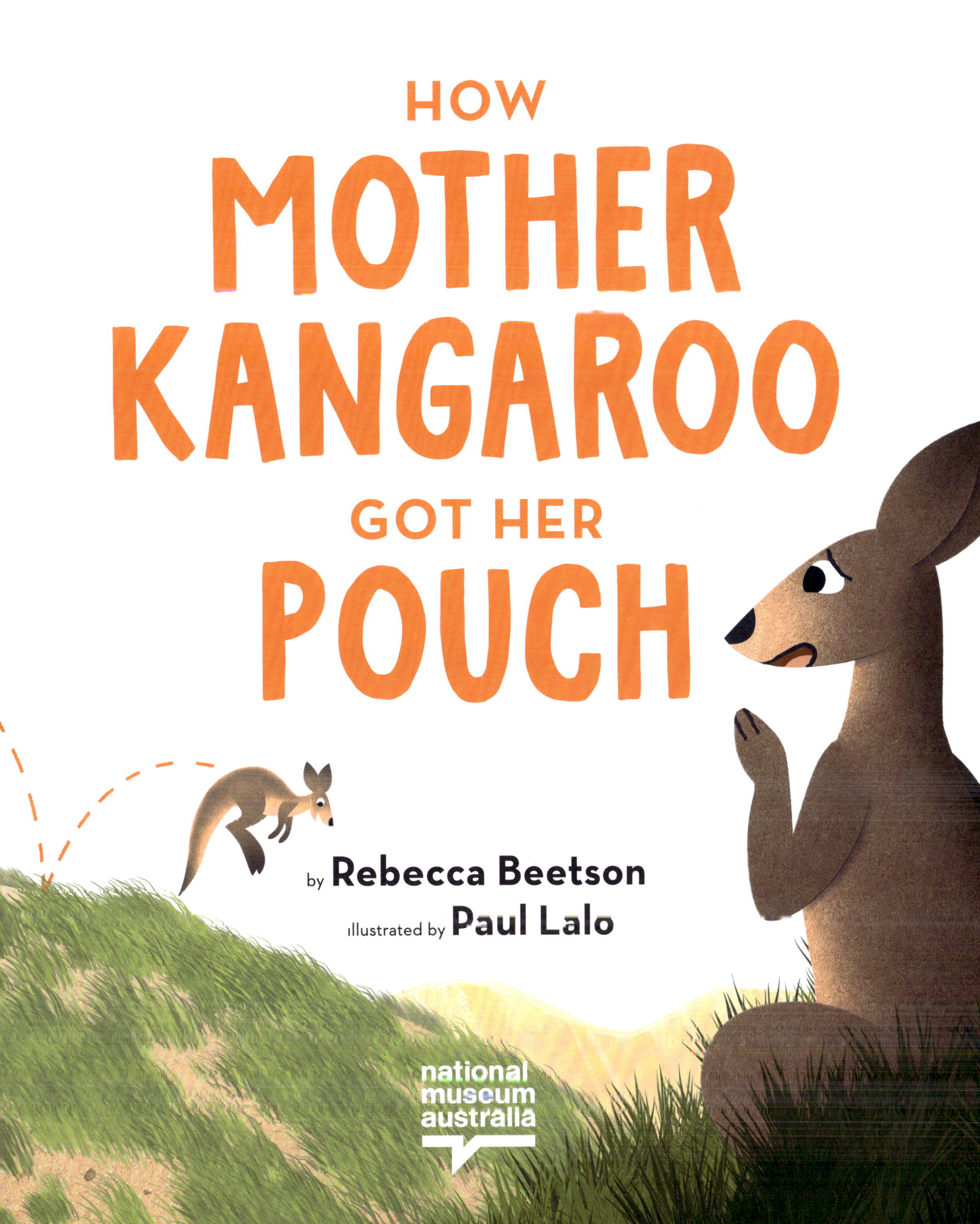

HOW MOTHER KANGAROO GOT HER POUCH

by **Rebecca Beetson**

illustrated by **Paul Lalo**

national museum australia

Mother Bunda's joey, Baabay, loved to play.

He loved to leap over anything big.

He loved to turn somersaults.

And he especially loved to snuggle up with his mother.

But Baabay often ended up playing too far away from Mother Bunda.

Then she would call out,
'Come back, Baabay! Stay close!'

One day while Baabay was playing, Old Wambad came along.

He said to Mother Bunda, 'I cannot see very well. Would you help me find some grass to eat and water to drink?'

‘Yes,’ said Mother Bunda. ‘I will help you. Hold on to my tail and I will take you to some grass to eat and some water to drink.’

As they went along, Baabay jumped ahead, going here and there.

'Come back, Baabay! Stay close!' Mother Bunda called out.

At the waterhole Old Wambad drank and drank and drank and Baabay splashed and splashed and splashed.

'Come back, Baabay! Stay close!' Mother Bunda called out.

At the grasslands the Old Wambad ate and ate and ate.

Baabay turned somersaults, bouncing and bouncing and bouncing.

'Come back, Baabay! Stay close!'
Mother Bunda called out.

'Thank you for being so kind to me,' smiled Old Wambad.

They settled under the shade of a tree to rest, but Mother Bunda sensed danger.

Hunters were about.

‘Stay here and hide.

I will lead the hunters away,’ she said.

Mother Bunda led the hunters far away ...

... over sandhills ...

... and across plains.

She hid in a cave and waited until the hunters gave up.

When she came back Baabay was alone under the tree.

Mother Bunda nudged Baabay awake.
'Where did Old Wambad go?'

Suddenly a spirit appeared in the sky.
Old Wambad was really Baayaami the creator spirit.

'For being so kind to me I would like to give you a gift,' Baayaami said.

Baayaami gave Mother Bunda a dillybag. As she tied the dillybag on …

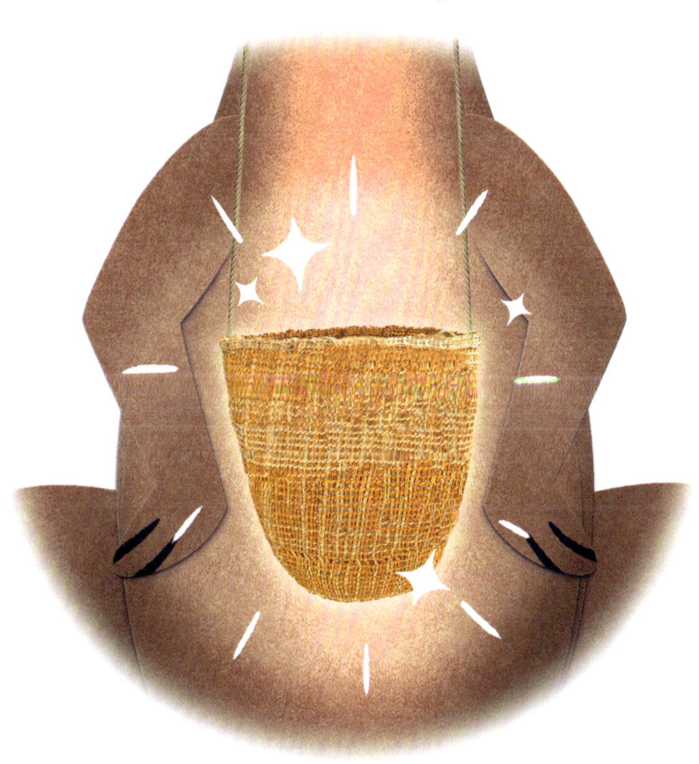

... it magically transformed into a pouch.

Now Mother Bunda had a way to keep Baabay close to her ...

… and they could snuggle
better than ever.

I dedicate this story to my children, and to all the children who help and go out of their way to be good people. Good things are coming your way.

— Rebecca Beetson Yaingayaingarra

The story

Rebecca Beetson is a Wiradjuri and Gamilaroi woman, author and artist. Yaingayaingarra, Rebecca's Aboriginal name, means 'To help'. Rebecca first heard the story of how the kangaroo got her pouch from a visiting artist at North Dubbo Public School. In Wiradjuri, Bunda means 'mother kangaroo', Baabay is 'joey' and Wambad is how we get the word 'wombat'.

The series

How Mother Kangaroo Got Her Pouch is the second in a series of five picture books featuring stories from Australia inspired by the Tim and Gina Fairfax Discovery Centre at the National Museum of Australia.

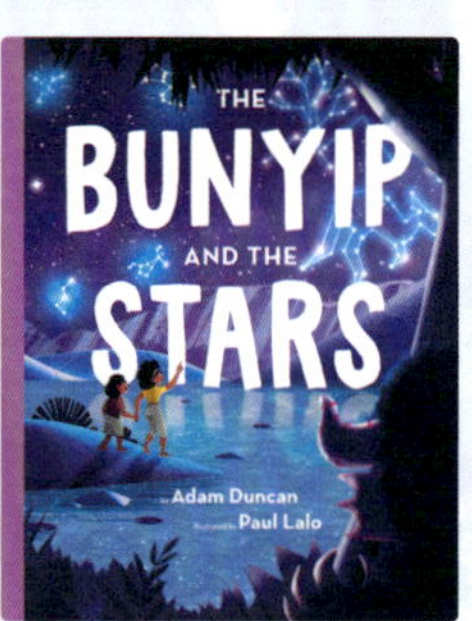

The first book in the series, *The Bunyip and the Stars* by Adam Duncan, is available from The Museum Shop shop.nma.gov.au.

Published by the National Museum of Australia Press on the lands of the Ngunnawal and Ngambri.
Printed in Australia on the lands of the Wathaurong.

Editor: Irma Gold
Designer: Anna McGregor
Illustrator: Paul Lalo, Soymilk Studio
Illustration concept designer: Jenni Vigaud
Printer: Adams Print
Typeset in Neutraface and Jealous Punk

A catalogue record for this book is available from the National Library of Australia.
978-1-921953-50-7

First published in 2024
National Museum of Australia Press
Lawson Crescent, Acton,
Canberra ACT 2601
Australia
publications@nma.gov.au